This book belongs to:

_____

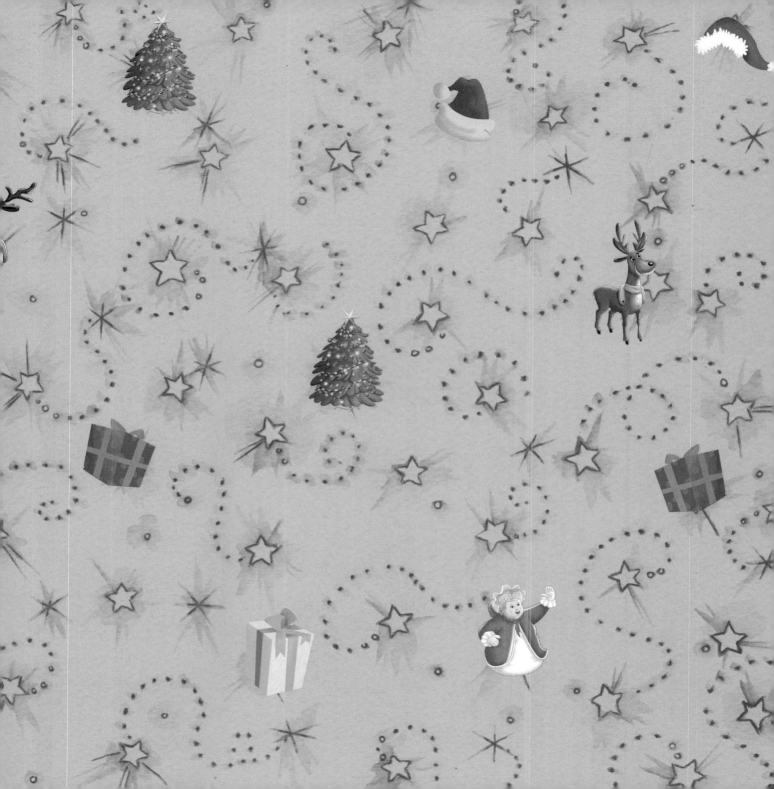

This book is dedicated to all children
who love to giggle!

I SAW SANTA'S UNDERPANTS

Written by Bobbie Hinman
Illustrated by Remesh Ram

Very late on that night...
just before Christmas day,

NORTH POLE

Santa swept all the dust
from his red Christmas sleigh.

He opened the closet, grabbed one of his suits,
and his shiny black belt, and his favorite black boots.

It was time to bring presents to good girls and boys,
so the elves packed the sack with gazillions of toys.

Then into the sleigh, Santa leaped like a frog,
as the snow filled the air with a thick, cold, white fog.
His reindeer were ready to make the big trip.
Bringing blankets and snacks, they were ready to rip.

Mrs. Claus stood there watching and waving goodbye, as the sleigh lifted up and flew into the sky.

Right after they left, she went back through the door,
and couldn't believe what she saw on the floor!

"He forgot his suspenders," she said with a frown.
"Without them, I fear that his pants will fall down!"

But Santa continued to fly without knowing...
that something that shouldn't be seen might be showing!

And way down below, a boy fixed a nice treat...
a plate filled with cookies for Santa to eat.

Max wished on a star to see Santa stop by,
then like magic, he saw the big sleigh in the sky.

The sound that Max heard,
he just knew was a hoof.
Cooper opened one eye and
let out a small *woof*.

Woof...

Then...
swoosh!
From the chimney, there came a loud noise,
and Santa appeared with a huge sack of toys.

He piled lots of presents right under the tree.
Max couldn't help thinking, *Which one is for me?*

Then suddenly, Santa grabbed onto his pants!
"My suspenders!" he cried. "Have I lost them by chance?"

Still clutching the sack, Santa's face wore a frown.
He couldn't let go or his pants would fall down!

Cooper opened both eyes
and came rushing to see...
Just who was this stranger
there under the tree?

"No, Cooper!" Max shrieked.
"No, Cooper! No! No!"
Cooper grabbed Santa's pants
and he wouldn't let go!

And then as it happened, Max took a quick glance,
and thats when he saw them...those striped underpants!

Max covered his eyes,
trying hard not to stare,
but not helping Santa
would be so unfair.

"No, you can't leave like that or you'll catch quite a cold.
I don't mean to be rude, but you are kinda old."

Then snatching the curtain, Max said, "This is it!"
But the size was all wrong and it just didn't fit.

And that's when Max realized that there on a hook,
were Mom's bright bandanas. They'd make a great look.

Max tied little knots.
Santa's face held a grin.
And then, here and there,
they just added a pin.

"It works!" shouted Santa.
"I can get on my way!"

So he headed back out and
climbed into his sleigh.

"No one will believe me. There isn't a chance!
But I know what I saw—Santa's striped underpants!"

If you enjoy this book—and I know you will—please tell your friends about it.

A review on Amazon is always appreciated.

Simply scan the code, or follow the link, and you will land on the review page.

Enjoy!

HTTPS://bit.ly/
underpants-review

For even more fun, you will love
these other books by Bobbie Hinman:

THE
BELLY
BUTTON
FAIRY
BY
BOBBIE HINMAN
ILLUSTRATED BY
MARK WAYNE ADAMS

THE
FART
FAIRY
BY
BOBBIE HINMAN
ILLUSTRATED BY
MARK WAYNE ADAMS

THE
FRECKLE
FAIRY
BY
BOBBIE HINMAN
ILLUSTRATED BY
MARK WAYNE ADAMS

THE
KNOT
FAIRY
BY
BOBBIE HINMAN
ILLUSTRATED BY
KRISTI BRIDGEMAN

THE
SOCK
FAIRY
BY
BOBBIE HINMAN
ILLUSTRATED BY
KRISTI BRIDGEMAN

Illustrations by Remesh Ram
Cover and Layout by Praise Saflor

For information: www.bestfairybooks.com

Names: Hinman, Bobbie, author. | Prayan Animation Studio, Ltd., illustrator. Title: I saw
Santa's underpants! / by Bobbie Hinman; [illustrated by Prayan Animation Studio,
Ltd.] Description: Kissimmee, FL: Best Fairy Books, 2022. | Summary: An inventive
boy helps Santa out of an embarrassing situation! Identifiers: LCCN: 2022910743 |
ISBN: 978-1-7365459-8-0 (hardcover) | 978-1-7365459-7-3 (paperback) Subjects:
LCSH Santa Claus--Juvenile fiction. | Christmas--Juvenile fiction. | Humorous stories. |
BISAC JUVENILE FICTION / General | JUVENILE FICTION / Holidays & Celebrations /
Christmas & Advent | JUVENILE FICTION / Humorous Stories Classification: LCC
PZ8.3.H5564 Is 2022 | DDC [E]—dc23

Best Fairy Books

Made in the USA
Middletown, DE
29 November 2022

16479356R00022